www.mascotbooks.com

The Boy Who Lost His Smile

For more information, please contact:
Mascot Books
560 Herndon Parkway #120
Herndon, VA 20170
info@mascotbooks.com

Library of Congress Control Number: 2016906018

CPSIA Code: PRT0616A
ISBN-13: 978-1-63177-643-4

Printed in the United States

THE BOY WHO LOST HIS SMILE

by Steve Wachtel • Illustrated by Luke Lawnicki

Johnny Peters was like any other boy. He collected creepy crawly bugs, little racing cars, and comic books, especially ones about his favorite character, Laughing Man.

What Johnny was really known for was his smile. It stretched from his right ear to his left and covered his whole face. But one morning, he woke up, ran to the mirror like he always did, and smiled. But nothing happened. Nothing, nada, zippo-the-hippo. *His smile was gone!*

He dressed and ran downstairs. "Mom,"
he said, "I need your help."

"What is it, Johnny?" she said.

"I woke up this morning and couldn't smile.
I still can't!"

"Of course you can," his mom laughed. "I'm making your favorite food, waffles! They always make you smile."

The smell of waffles tickled Johnny's nose and his belly grumbled, but he just could not smile.

Johnny ran to find his father. *He'll know what to do,* he thought.

"Dad," Johnny called. "I need—"

Bang! Mr. Peters hammered a nail hard.

"Dad!" Johnny cried louder.

"Oh! Hi, Johnny," said his dad. "You like this new doghouse I'm building for Ginger?"

"I need your help," said Johnny. "I've lost my smile!"

His dad frowned. Then he smiled and said, "I can fix anything, just wait one second."

"Ta-da!" said his dad, admiring his handiwork.
"Good as new."

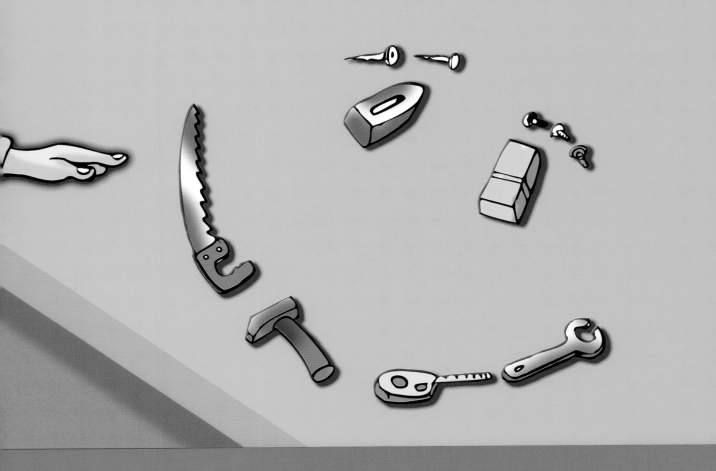

"Thanks, anyway, Dad," said Johnny.

A half hour later, Johnny joined his best friend Ray Elliot on the porch.

"Something's different about you, man," Ray said, shaking his head.

"Yeah," said Johnny. "I've lost my smile."

"Did you get in trouble with your parents?" Ray asked.

"No, nothing like that," Johnny said. "I just can't smile. Mom and Dad don't even believe me."

"Don't worry!" said Ray, springing to his feet. "I know what to do!"

"Let's ask Laughing Man!" Ray grinned.

"But he's only in the comic books," said Johnny.
"How's that gonna help?"

"He must know all the secrets of smiling, that's all he does!"
Ray explained. "Don't you have all of his comics?"

"Yeah," said Johnny. "In my room."

"Then, let's go!"

"Wow!" Ray exclaimed, "I don't even remember *this* one."

"Oh yeah," Johnny replied, nodding. "That was before he met Circus Man and lost the True Beacon. Kind of like how I lost my smile…"

The two boys spent the afternoon searching through as many comics as they could. They worked from the most recent issue all the way back to the very first one. But still no luck.

"Maybe we can write to him?" suggested Ray. "I think there's an address in the comic books."

"I guess it's worth a shot," said Johnny, pulling out paper and pen. He decided to go with paper that didn't have lines on it. It looked more grown up.

Two days later, Johnny still hadn't smiled. He checked the mirror every morning just in case and his mom made him his favorite waffles for breakfast hoping it would help. Ray ran out of jokes to tell him, but it didn't matter anyway, nothing was working.

It's gone, Johnny thought, *lost forever.* And worst of all, there was still no word from Laughing Man.

The next day after dinner, Johnny had dish duty. *This really won't help me smile,* Johnny thought with his hands buried in soap suds. His little sister Cindy was putting together a puzzle of her favorite cartoon character, Bonchat the Cat. *She's done that puzzle a million times,* he thought, *but look how happy she is. Wish that could be me.*

"Cindy," Mr. Peters said, "don't you ever get sick of that old puzzle? Let me see if I have any new ones you could work on. I'll be right back."

Suddenly, the doorbell rang. "I'll answer it," said Mrs. Peters, getting up. "Johnny, it's for you!"

Johnny couldn't believe his eyes!

"Well, Johnny," his mom said, "aren't you going to invite your friend in?"

"Oh yes, umm yeah," Johnny sputtered. "Please, sir, er- I mean, Mr. Laughing Man, please come in."

"I can't believe you're here," Johnny said, shaking his head. "Actually, well, er—"

"Actually you didn't believe I was real, right?" said Laughing Man, fixing Johnny with a stare.

Johnny lowered his head and nodded. He felt his lips begin to tremble.

"That's okay," boomed Laughing Man. "I didn't believe you were real either. Not too many boys lose their smiles."

"Can you help me?" Johnny sighed.

Laughing Man sprang into action. "I can fix anything!"
he cried. Then he circled Johnny once, twice, and finally
once more chanting,

"By the power of laughter,
By the True Beacon I vow,
Johnny's smile must return faster
than a wish, starting right now!"

Ten seconds went by, then fifteen, and Johnny waited to
feel something. But the sides of his mouth sat stubbornly,
refusing to rise. "Not even Laughing Man can help me,"
he whispered, sadly.

"Look!" Cindy cried out suddenly. "He's falling apart!" Then she burst into laughter.

Sure enough, the left side of Laughing Man's mask fell off and the right side drooped strangely sideways. Johnny was astonished.

Johnny suddenly felt his lips twitching. He couldn't help himself. A grin spread over his face and he broke out into loud laughter!

"Oh, Dad!" he sputtered. "You look so funny!"

Mr. Peters joined in the laughter. "Most of my fix-its fall apart," he said. "But I have a feeling this one worked!"

"Sure did!" Johnny laughed. Then he grinned the widest of them all.

About the Author

Steve Wachtel is a lifetime New Yorker who derives inspiration from the city's diversity and boundless energy. Mr. Wachtel grew up in Brooklyn and Long Island and was fortunate to be surrounded by loving family and friends who encouraged and supported the growth of his imagination. He has previously published three books of poetry before branching out to write his first children's book.

He was inspired to write this book by the second graders he has volunteered with for the last twelve years and continues to volunteer with today. By reading books with them, he hopes to share his strong love of reading and instill that love in their young minds.